Use your gifts to inspire the

Baked in Love,
Chef Amari-Lee
Ashalah Mechelle
& Dr Q Swift

Copyright © 2019 BakeOlogy 101: A Guide to Baking with S.T.E.A.M
Written By: Dr. Arkeria S. Wright, Ashalah Michelle Wright,
and Eugene "Amari-Lee" Goodson
Illustrated By: Chasity Hampton
Cover Design, Interior Design and Formatting: Whimsical Designs by CJ, LLC

All rights reserved. This book or any portion thereof may not be reproduced or used in any manner whatsoever without the express written permission of the publisher except for the use of brief quotations in a book review.

Printed in the United States of America.
ISBN: 9781072703679

First printing, 2019

DR. ARKERIA S. WRIGHT

P.O Box 162862

Atlanta, Ga. 30321

www.thechildrensadvocate.com

BAKE-OLOGY 101

A Recipe Book & Guide to Baking with S.T.E.A.M

Using the craft of baking to infuse culinary elements mixed with S.T.E.A.M to enhance and inspire future careers in

Science,

Technology,

Engineering,

Arts,

and Mathematics.

BAKING

BAKING has become a part of our family. When I started this business, I thought it would just be about enjoying something I love. But my family took hold of the vision for my life. Now, it has become "the place in which we love and grow together". Sometimes we have days where we bake all hours in the night for big events like weddings or festivals and we share stories and discover new things together. We get angry and then laugh at our mistakes together. We've also had many dance parties in the kitchen. As Oprah Winfrey would say, we have a lot of "Ah ha" moments as we bake our way to Paris, to college, and to our dreams.

First, I'll introduce my mom, **Dr. Arkeria S. Wright**, also known as our Momanger or The Professor. My mom attended Spelman College where she majored in Early Childhood Development. She loved science and worked at The Eckerd Drugstore as a Pharmacy Technician, amongst other jobs. She soon became a 3rd grade teacher, 7th grade reading and math coach, then a 4th grade science teacher, 5th grade science summer academy teacher, and last a 2nd grade teacher for Atlanta Public Schools. She went on to develop a service program for children through her nonprofit, WE Advocate, formerly Greater Giving Ministries, Inc. where she supplies food, academic tutoring, and other resources to students in need. She won awards for her teaching and philanthropy. Now she owns and operates The Children's Advocate (www.thechildrensadvocate.com) where she continues to advocate for not only her very own children but other amazing children as well. She advocates on the basis of education equality, parental support, and business ownership in the black community. What I most love about my mom's work is that she is beyond passionate about making sure kids know that they are valuable and their gifts will also make room for them in this world. She works with parents of children with special needs and parents facing special custodial circumstances. Parents come to her for best practices and successful strategies as it pertains to education, family life, and entrepreneurship. She is my brother and I's manager and biggest supporter. She believes that it is parent's responsibility to truly listen to their children's hearts, in order to feed their minds, so that they are guided toward their purposes. My mom credits her support of our family businesses to her belief and faith in God. Pretty awesome huh? I sure think so!

Secondly, there's my amazing brother, the BOSS, Eugene Amari-Lee Goodson. He is better known as Chef Amari-Lee, Chef Boss, or Mr. Cool. He is a distinguished gentleman and is very cool in his approach to life. He just sits back at times and soaks up information like a sponge. What's really cool is that he uses that information to plan out the life he wants for himself. At 6 years old my brother created his first vision board and each year it just got better and better. Chef Amari-Lee is now 9 years old and he has never stopped believing in the dreams he placed on his vision board. Chef began workings as Cook Me Up A Notch's sous chef at 7 years old. He credits the inspiration to cook and bake to me. But what's so amazing about my brother is that he still held on to all the other things he'd discovered about himself that had almost nothing to do with baking. As a baker, Chef Amari-Lee has had the opportunity of making desserts for thousands of people in our 3 years of business, we've even baked for the rich and famous. He has been introduced to so many amazing opportunities, won awards, participated in cooking demonstrations, taught baking classes, and so much more. Most importantly, he prides himself of being a member of this family business. He is in the process now of creating his own brand, Coolege Academy. Which will be a platform to inspire the youth that COOL is when you learn to be yourself. COOL is essentially who you are and who you were born to be. Your interests, your flaws, your uniqueness, your talents, YOU! Don't you just love that? I think it's so COOL!

Then, there's me! Your girl, Ashalah Michelle Wright, known to many as Chef Ashalah Michelle, The Pastry Princess of Atlanta, Young Mogul, and the Girl Boss herself. LOL! Honestly, I'm just a girl that had a dream at 12 years old to be this traveling pastry chef that bakes french pastries and eats them all herself (and possibly share them with my friends and family, too). It is what I believe to be my way of passing down a tradition to generations after me. A tradition of food that feeds the soul and brings happiness to your home. A tradition that speaks to dreams, and ambition, and belief in oneself. Since starting my business in February of 2016, I've won numerous awards for her delicious desserts, entrepreneurs efforts, as well as leadership skills. I've been interviewed and seen on various radio stations, tv programs, magazines, and podcast such as V-103, WAOK 1480, Atlanta LIVE Channel 54, The Rennie Curran Podcast, The Raising Entrepreneurs Podcasts, My Time Magazine, The Kids News Maker Magazine, Chione Magazine, JoJoPersonaliTV, The Ask Faris Show, and Dr. Nilda Perez Foresight Strategist Show.

I'll take over from here!

Ashalah uses her platform to inspire kids all around the world. In that effort, she is not only the President of Greater Giving Ministries, Inc Youth Services program where she supplies food and cooking lessons to kids in need during the holidays, she partners with various community organizations and nonprofits to effect change on a broader scale. She has partnered with The Black Chefs Network advocating for Black culinary excellence, I Am B.E.A.U.T.I.F.U.L, Inc. campaign sponsored by Lane Bryant, Young Mogul Market with Raising A Mogul Society, Morning Star International, Spark and Hustle with Aprille Franks-Hunt, Taste and Tell Expo benefiting mental health awareness, The Village Market ATL, H.Y.P.E 2016 & 2017 Youth Empowerment Summit Sponsor, Girls Who Brunch Tour Ambassador, & Young, Wealthy, Genius Ambassador amongst many more!

Her baking kits are now used during baking parties and Bakeology 101 workshop packages with Chef Ashalah. Ashalah has stood the course in business and philanthropy. Facing many different trails and losses. She has continued, since the age of 8 in given her time to initiatives surrounding child hunger and youth empowerment. She started her business from scratch as she taught herself to bake from YouTube. She credits her grandma for being her true inspiration. Her dreams have stretched beyond borders as she now strives to CAKE HER WAY TO PARIS and BEYOND. She assigns a portion of all cake sales toward traveling abroad, in hopes of learning from French Pastry Chefs, as well as to inspire kids all across the globe that their dreams are also worth S.T.E.A.M-ing toward!

When baking, I think about all we've learned in our classrooms about the Scientific Method. You know with the scientific method you begin with a purpose; a question based on the known or the unknown. The question here would be, how do we bake with Science, Technology, Engineering, ARTS, and Mathematics? Mmm! We also know that a huge part of baking is rooted in science. Furthermore, not only is science a great contributor to baking but so is technology, engineering, art, and a boatload of mathematics.

Our purpose for writing this book is to share with you an innovative and spectacularly fun way of teaching academic content areas by connecting everyday skills like baking to essentially increase student's confidence, mastery levels, and will to believe. This recipe book and S.T.E.A.M guide can be used both in your kitchens and in your classrooms.

Our plan for using this Bakeology 101 guide is to engage you in our world of S.T.E.A.M Baking as we infuse culinary arts with Science, Technology, Engineering, ARTS, and Mathematics.

SCIENCE

8

Science & Safety

Learning to properly handle food is one of the more important lessons and survival skills that we can sometimes overlook. Knowing how and what things are going into our bodies starts with proper hygiene. So little chefs, let's head over to the sink to wash our hands.

- ★ **Squeeze** a small pea-size amount of hand soap into your hands.
- ★ **Lather** under warm water by rubbing hand together for at least 20 seconds.
- ★ **Dry** your hands with a dry cloth.
- ★ **READY TO BAKE!**

READ all instructions listed on recipe card before you begin the fun!

WASH your hands, kitchen surfaces, and baking tools with warm soapy water before using.

STORE all perishables food in the appropriate storage space at the right temperature.

CLEAN as you go! If you spill ingredients on the floor or on countertops, clean up immediately to avoid any slip-ups or contamination.

USE oven gloves or cloths to remove hot pots from the stovetop or baking pans from the oven. Be careful of steam or hot air when you open the oven door. Place hot food on a stable, heat-resistant surface.

STORE any leftovers in the refrigerator for up to 4 days. After 4 days, it should be discarded in the trash! Cake, Frosting, and cookie batters can be frozen for longer periods of time (always do your research on storage rules based on the ingredients used in your dish).

NOW, LET'S INVESTIGATE!

BAKEOLOGY

SCIENCE - TECHNOLOGY - ENGINEERING - ARTS - MATHEMATIC

S.T.E.A.M INVESTIGATION: SALT-VS-SUGAR

Baking Crystals: Macroscopic & Microscopic Finds

SALT   SUGAR

BAKING WITH SALT AND SUGAR

Have you ever wondered why salt is needed in pastry recipes? The main function of salt in cake recipes is to enhance the flavor of the other ingredients. Its presence perks up the depth and complexity of other flavors as the ingredients meld. Salt also provides a balance to the sweetness of cake batters. Sugar, however, contains an amino acid that starts the caramelizing aldehyde. Aldehyde is an organic compound containing the CHO (Carbohydrate). Without sugar, flour proteins cannot join in the baking process and make gluten which helps the cake/dough to rise.

Did you know? We need a constant supply of sugar in our diets. Our cells rely on sugar as their primary source of energy and function at a laggardly pace without it. If sugar is not preferred, you will need to find another source of energy to put in its place!

Can you tell the difference? **Take a look!**

MATERIALS NEEDED:
- ★ Microscope or Magnifying Hand Lens
- ★ Plain glass slides
- ★ Unlabeled salt and sugar
- ★ Polarizing film or the lenses from some polarizing sunglasses (optional)

○ **What do you predict?**
_____
_____

What tool did you choose?
_____
_____

What do you see?
_____
_____
_____

NOW LET'S SEE HOW THESE TWIN LOOK-ALIKES CRYSTALS INTERACT.
This simple experiment shows us a way in which salt and sugar react to water.
- ★ Pour 1 teaspoon of salt into a clear plastic cup and 1 teaspoon of sugar into another clear plastic cup
- ★ Add 1/3 cup of warm water to each, stir for 10 seconds and wait for 3 minutes.
- ★ Observe the interaction.

○ **What do you see?**
_____
_____

YOU MAY FIND THAT THE SALT CRYSTALS DIDN'T INTERACT WITH THE WATER AT ALL, BUT THE SUGAR CRYSTALS FORMED INTO A STICKY FOAM.

WHAT'S HAPPENING:
As the water evaporates, the salt or sugar atoms join together to form regular patterns. These patterns are different depending on what substances they are made from. When crystals are viewed with polarized light, they split the light into different colors. This makes them easier to see and helps scientists identify what type of crystals they are based on the colors they have.

Find more activities like these at http://sciencing.com

Now, let's use salt and sugar in our first recipe!

○ *Now, let's cook things up a notch!*

Cook Me UP A Notch
Cookies, Cakes, and Culinary Creations

Homemade Classic Yellow Cake

Ingredients

- 2 cup all-purpose flour
- 1 teaspoon baking powder
- 1 teaspoon baking soda
- ½ teaspoon salt
- 1½ cup granulated sugar
- 1 cup unsalted butter (2 sticks), softened, do not melt
- 2 eggs, room temperature
- 2 yolks, room temperature
- 2 teaspoons butter-vanilla emulsion
- 1 teaspoon butter flavoring (optional)
- 1 cup buttermilk, room temperature

PREP TIME: 15 minutes
TOTAL TIME: 25 minutes
SERVING SIZE: One 2-layer cake

INSTRUCTIONS
1. Preheat oven to 325 F.
2. Grease and lightly flour, round 9-inch cake pans. Set aside.
3. In a medium-size bowl, whisk together flour baking powder, baking soda, and salt. Set aside.
4. In a mixing bowl cream together, sugar and butter.
5. Mix in eggs and yolks, one at a time, mixing after each egg.
6. Mix in butter-vanilla emulsion and butter flavoring.
7. Add the dry ingredients into the wet ingredients, alternating with the buttermilk.
8. Mix until batter is fluffy, being sure to scrape down the sides of the bowl. (batter will be thick)
9. Let batter rest for 5 minutes.
10. Pour batter evenly into prepared pans and use an offset spatula to spread into an even layer.
11. Bake for 30-35 minutes (may need a tad bit longer) or until golden around the edges and moist crumbs cling to a toothpick inserted into the center.
12. Place on a cooling rack until pans are warm enough to touch and then carefully remove cake from pans and allow to cool completely.
13. Frost with chocolate frosting or any icing you desire.

Finding the perfect classic yellow cake recipe is a perfect start to baking. This cake can be used by adding or subtracting one or two ingredients to change the flavor of the cake. I would call this cake a base or foundation cake.

The Georgia Peach Cobbler Pound Cake

Ingredients
- 2 Georgia Peaches, peeled and pureed
- 3 cups all-purpose flour, sifted
- 3 cups granulated sugar
- 6 large eggs
- 3 ½ sticks of margarine (1¾ cups)
- 2 teaspoons vanilla extract
- 2 teaspoons rum flavoring
- ½ cup creme cheese

PREP TIME: 45 minutes
TOTAL TIME: 1 hour and 15 minutes
SERVING SIZE: One Bundt Cake

Directions

1. Preheat oven to 325 F.
2. Grease and flour a Bundt pan lightly. Set aside.
3. Cream together butter and sugar.
4. Add crème cheese.
5. Mix in eggs one at a time.
6. Mix in vanilla extract and rum flavoring.
7. Add flour to the mixture (one cup at a time) until evenly combined.
8. Fold in pureed peaches. (use spatula)
9. Spoon batter into prepared pan.
10. Bake for 1 hour and 15 minutes (check it at the 1-hour mark)
11. Let cake cool in pan until pan is warm to the touch.
12. Remove cake from pan and let finish cooling on a cooling rack.

Vanilla Glaze

1. Mix together ½ cup powdered sugar, 1 teaspoon vanilla, tablespoon condensed milk. (may need more milk for glaze consistency.

2. Drizzle glaze on top of the cake. Be sure to make crumble before drizzling. Sprinkle a little crumble on the top of the glaze.

3. Let glaze harden and serve with vanilla ice cream.

Crumble

1. Mix 1 teaspoon ground cinnamon, 1 teaspoon ground nutmeg, 2 teaspoon vanilla extract, ½ cup sugar, 3 2/3 cup flour, 1 ½ cup unsalted butter

2. Place mixture on a flat pan

3. Bake for 15 minutes at 350 degrees Fahrenheit

4. Let cool then sprinkle on the cake after applying glaze

THE BACKSTORY

"For me, it started with a pound cake — one that was passed down from generation to generation. The lemon pound cake is a southern favorite and one of the first cakes I learned to bake. I was taught by my great aunt who was also taught by her aunt. Her aunt was my great-great aunt and my mom's adopted mom. I know it sounds a bit confusing. To make it simple, it's my grandmother's recipe. I then taught my daughter, Chef Ashalah, and Ashalah taught Chef Amari-Lee. It was our introduction to "made-from-scratch" cake baking. But, every good baker adds a twist of their own to the classic recipes. Thus, we decided to take this traditional, classic pound cake recipe and turn it up a notch by adding some delicious, sweet Georgia peaches."

TECHNOLOGY

Technology is a big part of today's world. We use it for almost EVERYTHING! Generation Z is the most innovative and creative technology enhancers of all time. We are a group of savvy, cool inventors! We use technology in many ways. One of such ways is through the social media. Tech applications like Instagram, Facebook, Periscope, Twitter, YouTube, Snapchat, and so many more allow us access to the world beyond our reach. We are able to send real-time media to people all over the world with just the touch of a button. We share our lives, learn from others, and promote our businesses. We can attach sound to videos or even add movement to images. We can use Twitter to pen pal a new friend in China or in Africa. We share vibrant pictures, disappearing videos, or even post advertisements on Instagram and Snapchat. We can teach baking classes or start social campaigns on Periscope that we love. Facebook Live and IG TV are great tools, and even YouTube. I especially enjoy engaging in professional development online because it is convenient and it's always important to continue to enhance one's skills. The world is our oyster, people!

Technology & Training

Technology has created opportunities for so many new inventions that have helped this world advance in so many incredible ways. Before there were computers and cell phones, social media, and downloadable apps, there were scientists, creating tools with only their own brilliance and as much as their hands could craft. Because of them, we have so many assistive devices to make our lives easier. Because of the foundation they laid, we are able to build on and expand their original ideas and innovate beyond their ever imagined measures.

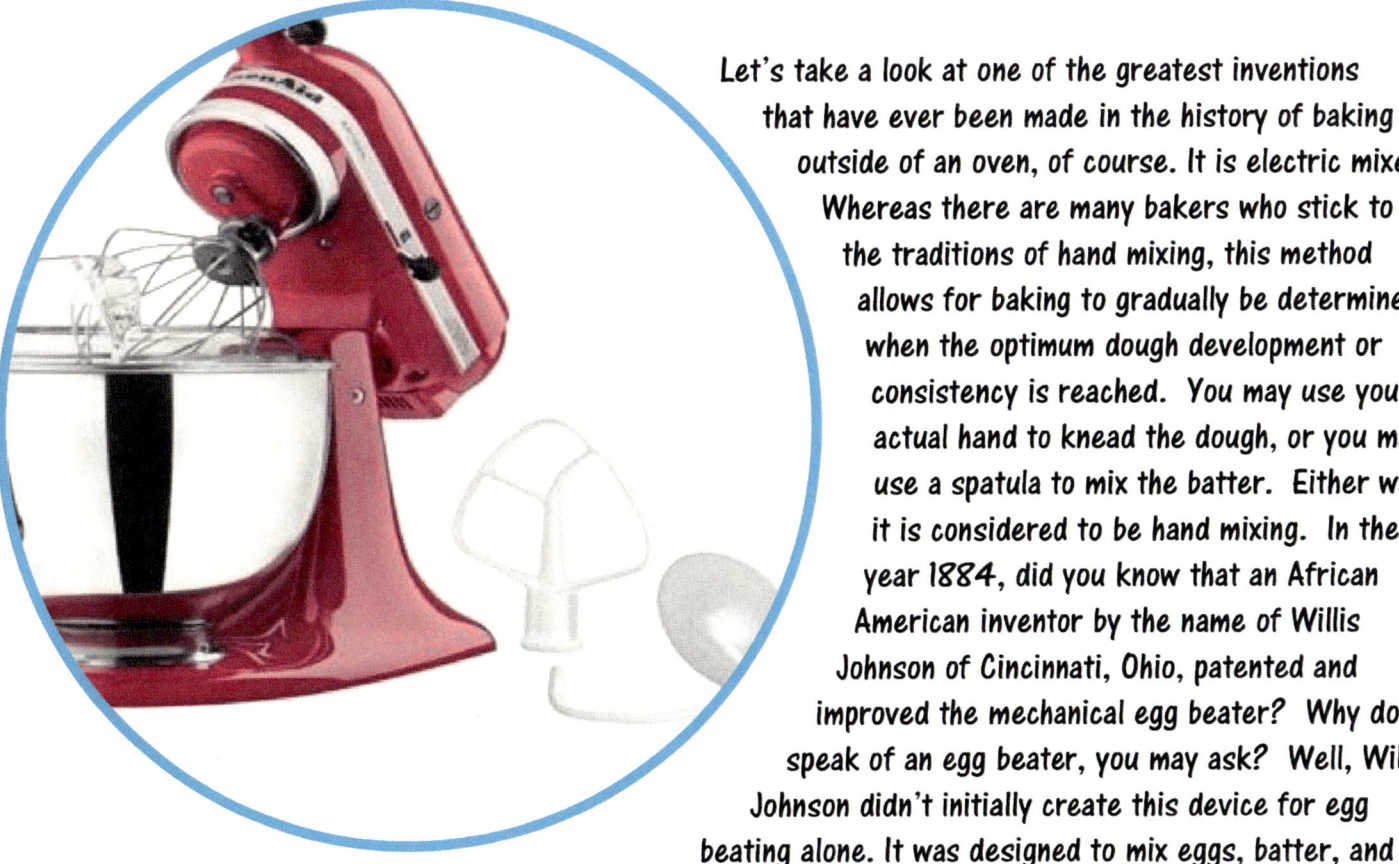

Let's take a look at one of the greatest inventions that have ever been made in the history of baking outside of an oven, of course. It is electric mixer! Whereas there are many bakers who stick to the traditions of hand mixing, this method allows for baking to gradually be determined when the optimum dough development or consistency is reached. You may use your actual hand to knead the dough, or you may use a spatula to mix the batter. Either way, it is considered to be hand mixing. In the year 1884, did you know that an African American inventor by the name of Willis Johnson of Cincinnati, Ohio, patented and improved the mechanical egg beater? Why do I speak of an egg beater, you may ask? Well, Willie Johnson didn't initially create this device for egg beating alone. It was designed to mix eggs, batter, and other baker's ingredients.

What makes it power on and off? Electromagnets are used in devices to turn things on and off. When the switch is turned on the current from the wire creates an electric flow. The object connected to the wire becomes a magnet that sends the current from the spinning coil to metal rings.
Then, PRESTO your MIXING THINGS UP A NOTCH!

At Cook Me Up A Notch, we are so thankful for this invention because it has made a life of baking so much easier. This invention has made room for other mixers, such as the stand mixer or another name is the vertical mixer.

Brown Butter Sweet Potato Pie

Ingredients

FOR CRUST:
- 1 cup all-purpose flour
- 1/8 teaspoon salt
- 1/3 cup cold salted butter, cut into chunks
- 3 to 4 tablespoons cold water

1. Heat oven to 350°F.
2. Combine flour and 1/8 teaspoon salt in a bowl; cut in butter with pastry blender or fork until mixture resembles coarse crumbs. Stir in enough water with fork just until flour is moistened. Shape into ball; flatten slightly.
3. Roll out ball of dough on lightly floured surface into 12-inch circle. Fold into quarters. Place dough into 9-inch pie pan; unfold, pressing firmly against bottom and sides. Trim crust to 1/2 inch from the edge of the pan. Crimp or flute edge. Set aside.

FOR FILLING:
- 1 ready-made deep-dish pie crust (or make your own crust-see above)
- ½ cup salted butter, cut into cubes or slices
- 2 lb. sweet potatoes washed (equals about 2 cups pureed)
- ½ cup light brown sugar, packed
- 1 cup granulated sugar
- ½ cup condensed milk
- 2 eggs, room temperature
- 1 teaspoon vanilla extract
- ½ teaspoon cinnamon
- ½ teaspoon nutmeg
- tiny pinch of lemon or orange zest (optional)
- 2 Tablespoons flour

PREP TIME: 35 minutes
TOTAL TIME: 20 minutes
SERVING SIZE: 2 Pies

Directions

1. Preheat oven to 350 F.
2. Place potatoes in a pot and cover with water. Boil potatoes until a fork can slide through with no difficulty (approximately 45 minutes)
3. When potatoes are tender, pour the water off potatoes and rinse with cold water to cool potatoes. (I personally like to peel and mix while hot, but it can be pretty hot so be careful if you do the same)
4. Place potatoes in large bowl and peel skin off potatoes.
5. Use a fork and divide sweet potatoes several pieces. (set aside)
6. Let cool while preparing the brown butter.
7. To make the brown butter, add butter to a heavy-bottom skillet over medium heat (brown butter burns FAST so keep a close watch, if taste like smoke throw it out and start over).
8. Once butter has melted it will begin to foam a bit, whisk continuously while scraping the bottom of the pan.
9. The butter will begin to turn golden and form golden brown bits on the bottom of the pan, keep whisking.
10. Once the aromas become nutty (almost like the smell of caramel) and the solids in the bottom of the pan are golden brown remove from heat.
11. Pour into a glass dish (including the brown solids) and set aside to let cool.
12. In large bowl with sweet potatoes, combine condensed milk, granulated sugar, brown sugar, vanilla extract, nutmeg, cinnamon, lemon zest (option) and flour. Mix on medium speed for 5 minutes or until smooth. Mix in the cooled brown butter until creamy and smooth.
13. Before adding egg, taste your mixture to ensure desired taste. If necessary, adjust your spices. If necessary, add a few splashes of water (or whole milk) until you have the texture of a very thick puree. (don't get it too watery, just use enough water/milk to make mixing easier)
14. Place ready-made pie crust in the oven for 3 minutes or until lightly golden.
15. Pour sweet potato mixture into pie crust shell and smooth the top.
16. Bake in oven on middle rack for 55 minutes.
17. Remove from oven and let cool completely until the middle is firmly set.
18. Enjoy cold or warm. Refrigerate leftovers.
19. Serve with sweetened whipped cream or vanilla ice cream.

ENGINEERING

20

ENERGY & ENGINEERING

Energy is everywhere!

We use it in our homes, in our cars, at school, as we play, and as we breath. Energy can be light, motion, heat, sound, fuel, or electricity. As a parent, we are always very conscious about how we use energy. We yell, "Turn off those lights, the sun is out!" We tell our kids, "To take good showers, not long showers." We complain about gas prices and devise ways to eliminate driving. And as our energy is restored for a long night of rest, we are depleted of energy as we exert ourselves living out our purposes each day. Although energy is in constant use every second of our day, energy cannot be destroyed but it can indeed be changed. How can energy change?

1st Lets take a look at the sun. The energy from the sun helps living things grow, right? Yes! The trees store energy in its parts, its leaves, branches, and trunk. When a tree is cut down, that energy is still present in its parts. We use the trunk or wood logs to build our campfires. Those wood logs become fuel because of the stored energy from the sun. We may use another source of fire (such as matches or a lighter) or even rub two sticks together to cause friction (which is an energy heat source). Once the fire comes in contact with our wood log, it ignites and causes the log to burn. Now, that our campfire is blazing let's practice using energy with my favorite recipe that I do with my kids!

Cook Me UP A Notch
Cookies, Cakes, and Culinary Creations

Chocolate-Covered Strawberry S'mores

INGREDIENTS NEEDED:

Honey Graham Crackers
Hershey Chocolate Candy Bars
Large Marshmallows
Fresh Strawberries (or choose the fruit you like best with chocolate)
Tin Plate or Pan

TOOL: USE A LONG STICK FROM TREE (SEARCH FOR A THIN BRANCH FROM THE TREE)

Instructions

1. **Prepare** a campfire (or fire in your fireplace). Allow the fire to simmer down so the logs are red hot rather than a roaring fire of flames.
2. **Break** one long graham cracker in half horizontally to make two squares. Slice one strawberry in 4 thin slices and lie flat on the graham cracker. Break the chocolate bar and place flat on top of strawberries, leaving the other graham cracker square open to use as the top. Set aside.
3. **Place** a marshmallow on a stick and hold it over the heat, rotating often, until the marshmallow is golden brown (or dark brown or burnt, if you prefer!) and the inside is gooey.
4. **Remove** the marshmallow from the fire and place it on top of the chocolate. Top the marshmallow with the second graham cracker square. Eat it sandwich style and enjoy taking the classic treat up a notch!

BAKEOLOGY

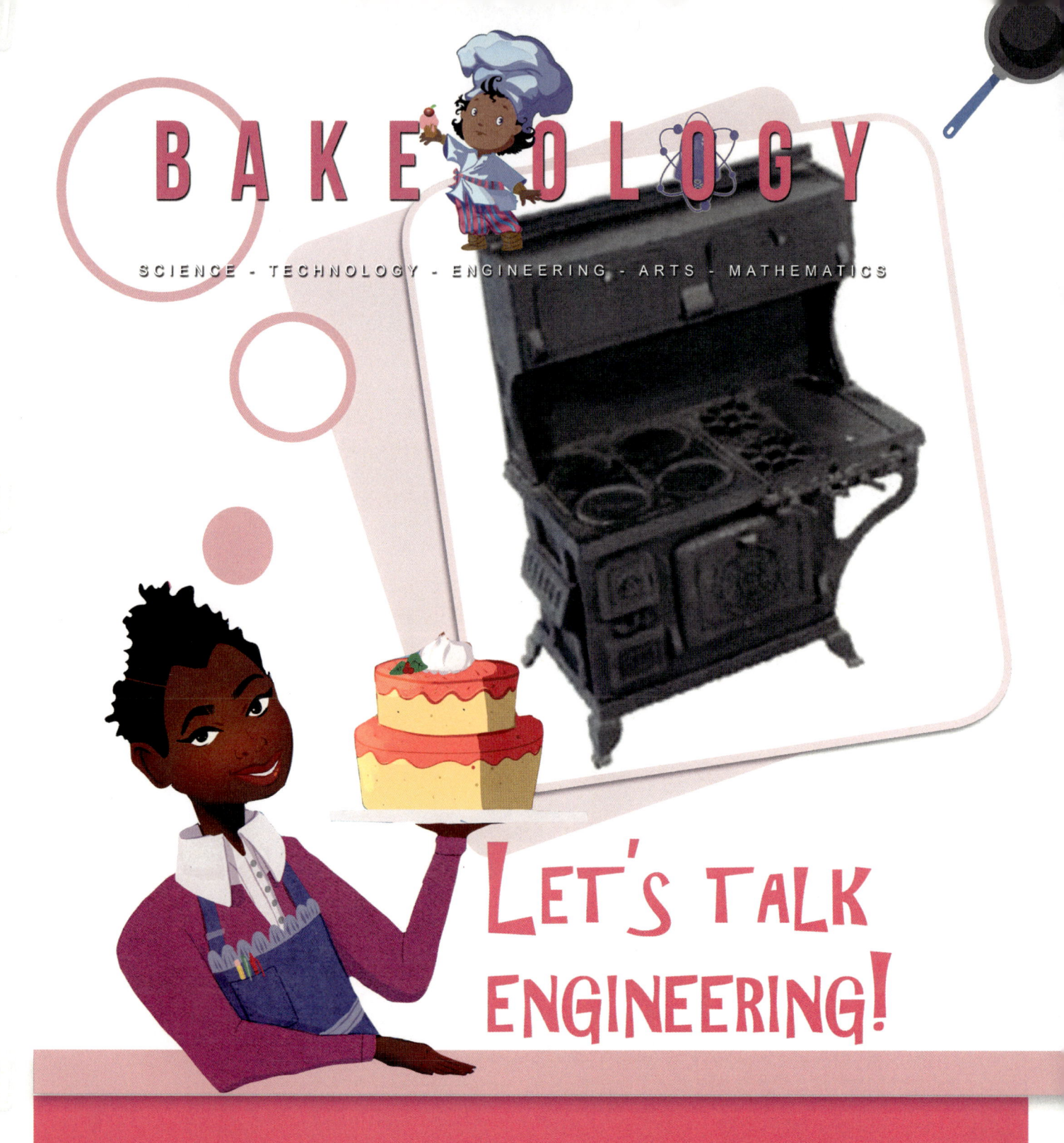

SCIENCE - TECHNOLOGY - ENGINEERING - ARTS - MATHEMATICS

Let's talk engineering!

FUN FACTS YEAR 1490: The first oven recorded in history was engineered in France, made of brick and tile. While there may have been others before this, the French oven is the first on the books. Over the years we have evolved from wood burning stoves/ovens, coal, to electric stove/ovens.

24

Let's Talk:
Thermal energy and how it is used in BAKING!!!

A few things can happen when you bake a cake. Some chemical reactions to keep in mind while doing this tasty experiment are:

- Heat helps baking powder produce tiny bubbles of gas, which makes the cake light and fluffy.
- Heat causes protein from the egg to change and make the cake firm.

Egg whites are almost made up of proteins. These proteins breakdown when heat is applied

Baking powder releases carbon dioxide twice during the entire baking process -- once when it hits water and once when it reaches a certain temperature in the oven.

Now watch an amazing YouTube video called "The Chemistry of Cookies" https://youtu.be/n6wpNhyreDE and complete the Engineering Section in your Bakeology 101 Workbook.

HOW DO BAKERS SAVE ENERGY?

We use so many sources of energy as bakers, so it is very important that we know how we can also help to save energy. By saving energy, you also save the Earth! Here's how.....

1. Make a grocery list before driving to stores, farmer's markets, or local farms like me to combine errands. This saves on fuel because you won't need to go back out for things you forgot. Or in my case, send my mom back out for things I forgot. EEEK! Oh, and don't forget your reusable bags instead of plastic bags.
2. Turn off lights or unplug gadgets, games, or devices that are constantly using power although it's powered off.
3. Avoid leaving the refrigerator open, the oven powered on when not in use, lights on during the day time, or water running in the sink.

For more information on energy for kids visit www.eere.energy.gov/kids/ , www.eia.doe.gov/kids/ , and www.need.org/energyfair.php

BAKEOLOGY

SCIENCE - TECHNOLOGY - ENGINEERING - ARTS - MATHEMATICS

Let's Bake: Culinary Engineering!

This recipe I truly love because most people that I've shared these cookies with can't believe that they are made from all-natural ingredients and much healthier than the standard chocolate cookie but just as delicious. The vanilla powder gives it a punch of flavor that fills your mouth with so much goodness.

Please check out my feature on www.yayastars.com and her review of these delicious cookies in the section "Favorite Things".

RECIPE: DELICIOUS ORGANIC CHOCO-CHIP COOKIES

PREP TIME: 20 MINUTES
COOK TIME: 12 MINUTES
TOTAL TIME: 32 MINUTES
SERVINGS: MAKES 24 COOKIES

BAKING TOOLS/MATERIALS NEEDED: MIXER, SPATULA, MIXING BOWL, COOKIE TRAY, AND PARCHMENT PAPER

Ingredients

1 1/2 cup(s) unsalted butter (softened to room temperature)
1 1/4 cup(s) organic sugar
1 1/4 cup(s) brown sugar, packed
1 Tbsp organic vanilla powder
2 large eggs*
4 1/2 cup(s) all-purpose unbleached flour
2 1/2 Tsp baking soda
1 Tsp salt
1 cup ground flax seeds
20 Oz H-E-B Organics Semi-Sweet Chocolate Chips (50% cocoa)

*Substitution: Vegan Butter, Egg Replacer

Instructions

1. Preheat oven to 350°F (176.667°C)
2. Cream butter, organic sugars and organic vanilla powder together in a large mixing bowl, beat in eggs or egg replacers.
3. In a separate mixing bowl combine organic flour, organic baking soda, ground flax seeds, and salt.
4. Add flour mixture to butter mixture in 3 separate batches, combining thoroughly each time.
5. Add organic semi-sweet chocolate chips once flour is completely mixed through.
6. Roll into 1-inch balls, place on baking pan and flatten slightly. Cook for 11 – 12 minutes, or until golden brown and still soft.

Art Bakeology

SCIENCE - TECHNOLOGY - ENGINEERING - ARTS - MATHEMATICS

FOOD COLORING: ARTISTRY & CHEMISTRY
S.T.E.A.M EXPERIMENT: BUBBLING WONDERS LAVA LAMP

Did you know...

Food coloring is made up mostly of water, and water has surface tension, meaning it clings to itself. Oil, however, is hydrophobic, meaning it doesn't mix well with water. This experiment will show you what happens when oil, water, and food coloring interact.

MATERIALS NEEDED...
3/4 cup of water
Funnel
A clean 1-liter bottle
Vegetable Oil
Food coloring
1 or 2 Effervescent Tablets

What's Happening:

The atoms that make up the outer layer of the food coloring won't bond with the oil. When you drop the effervescent tablets into the water, it begins to react, resulting in a lot of carbon dioxide gas. These gas bubbles rise to the surface, but once they hit the oil layer, the dense water sinks back down again, creating a lava lamp of moving bubbles! Effervescent tablets or carbon tablets are tablets which are designed to dissolve in water, and release carbon dioxide. In baking we use yeast, baking soda, or baking powder at create these carbon dioxide bubbles that helps the dough rise. When adding food coloring to your cake/dough mixer make sure to use less when using liquid food coloring which is more water based than gel or powder. Consider how oil and water chemistry works. The liquid food color can water down your cake compromising your batter. Be sure to use exact measurements for a vibrant masterpiece!

Art Education

Someone once said that "an art education helps build academic skills and increase academic performance, while also providing alternative opportunities to reward the skills of children who learn differently." I too believe that art education make room for children to explore their gifts. Those very gifts that live in each and every one of you. I believe that help define who you are and the tool you will use to drive your purpose. Most times I tell children that they can identify it when there's feeling inside themselves that get very excited about a thing, idea, or service. Or it can be something, idea, or service you find disrupts something inside you and causes a frustration, a need to advocate, or shows up as a problem that you are drawn to fix.

Yes, like The Professor said, just look inside yourself and allow your self-expression to come out. When I was 7 years old, I drew a picture of Iron Man and put it up for sale. I used my interest and created revenue for myself. Even though my pictures were only $2 each, it was a product I created, and it was fun to make money off of my very own talents. When baking I am able to create new flavors, shapes, and colors first with my artistic mind and heart, then it shows up with the desserts I prepare. Chef Mom also says that true artist doesn't have to choose one thing to be in life.

BE YOU!

Honor Roll Student & T-shirt Designer

Male Print Model & Business Owner of My Brand, Coolege Academy

Giver
&
Nonprofit
Vice-President
of
Youth Services

Sous Chef of
Cook Me Up a Notch
& Jr. Chef

31

Red Velvet Cupcake Dreams

Ingredients

- 2 ½ cups flour
- 1 ½ sugar
- 2 eggs (room temperature)
- 1 teaspoon cocoa powder
- 1 cup buttermilk (room temperature)
- 1 1/2 cup vegetable oil
- 1 tablespoon food coloring
- 1 teaspoon red velvet flavoring
- 1 teaspoon vanilla
- 1 teaspoon distilled vinegar

PREP TIME: 15 minutes
TOTAL TIME: 40 minutes
SERVING SIZE: 12 cupcakes

Instructions:

1. Preheat oven to 350 Fahrenheit. Line Muffin Pan with cupcake liners.
2. In medium bowl, whisk together flour, sugar, baking soda, salt, and cocoa powder.
3. In a large bowl, gently beat together the oil, buttermilk, eggs, food coloring, vinegar, and vanilla extract with a mixer.
4. Add the sifted dry ingredients to the wet and mix until smooth and thoroughly combined.
5. Pour cupcakes batter 2/3 filled into cupcake pans. Bake in oven for about 20-22 minutes, turning the pans once. Test the cupcakes with a toothpick to make sure it's done. Remove from the oven and cool completely before frosting.

GET ARTSY!

Icing: Choose your favorite cream cheese icing and add coloring or try the homemade cream cheese icing exclusively in my book, THE CITY OF DREAMS: ATLANTA www.cookmeupnaotch.com to get your hard copy or e-book!

BAKEOLOGY

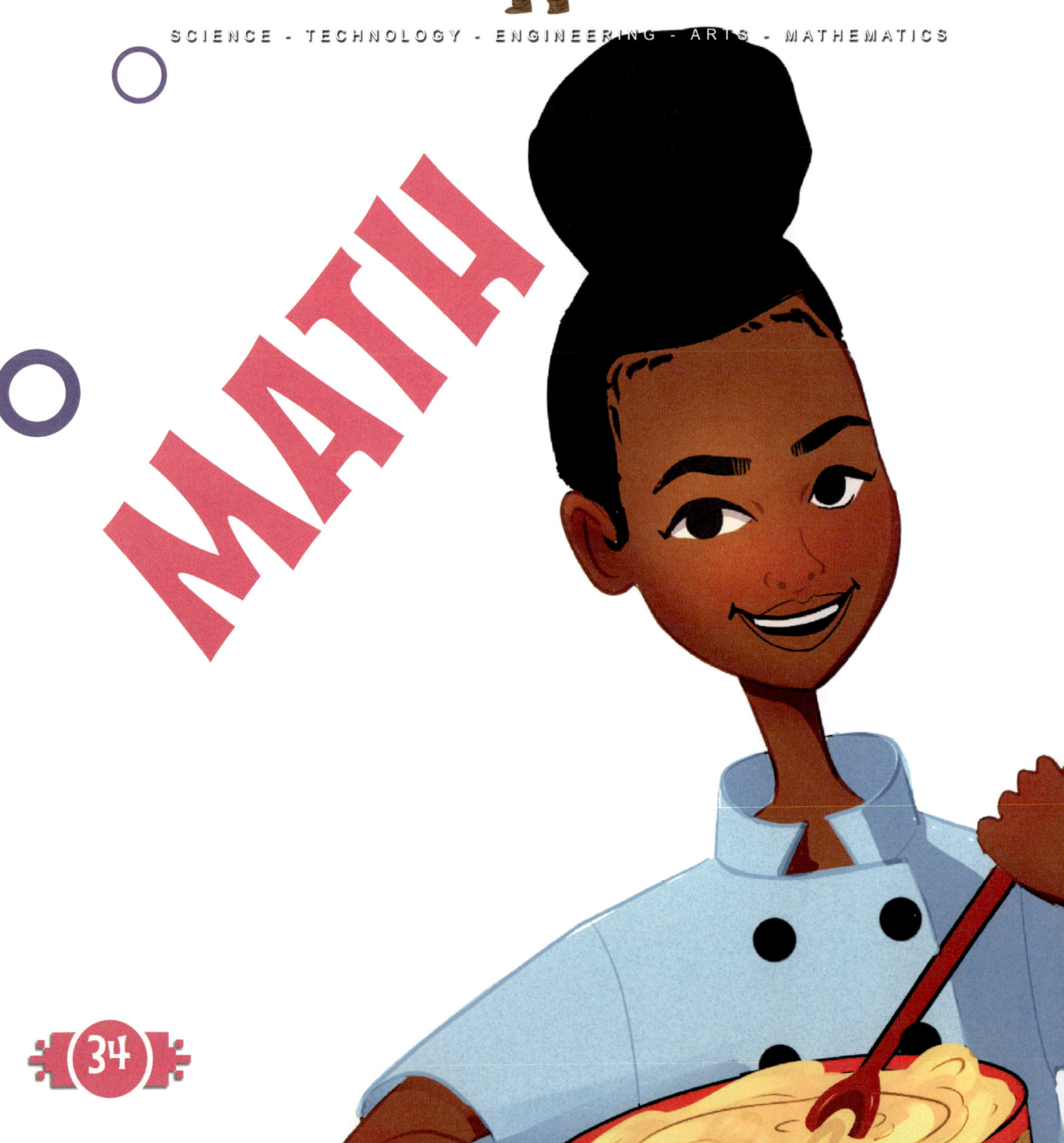

SCIENCE - TECHNOLOGY - ENGINEERING - ARTS - MATHEMATICS

MATH

34

MATH & MONEY

Baking accesses so many of the math skills we use each day, in such a fun and yummy way. During our baking sessions we use this opportunity to introduce and review measurement, fractions and percentages, per unit pricing, budget, profits & loss, and so much more. My little chefs light up most when we tell them that they can make a lot of money baking the sweets they love. See, I started my business after "testing" out my desserts at school. I decided a year before conduct a little market research and learn to bake the desserts my peers loved. After teaching myself to bake from YouTube, I couldn't wait for my classmates to try them. After about a year of transporting my baked goods in a "top-secret" lunch bag, I decided to create order forms because of such high demands for my desserts. I decided my first order will be for the upcoming holiday, Valentine's Day. I used the skills I had learned from a Business and Computer Science class and created an order form to prepare for upcoming sales. I shared the order form with my peers and collected their money for Valentine Sweetheart cupcakes and cookies. In doing this order form, I had to price how much it would cost me to make each cupcake and also the price of materials I would need for packaging them. I sold the cupcakes at $4 each and it would include a special note written for their sweetheart. When I returned home with the order form, I told my mom I had cupcake orders to make for Valentine's Day. She refused to believe that the students would pay me for my products. I then assured her they would by showing her that the orders were pre-ordered, and I had collected full payments from all of my customers. She was SHOCKED! I had to pitch my business to my mom first, seriously! This was my very first business decision and one of my best financial decisions I've had to make. I was able to make sure the funding was present to deliver the quality products that I had promised my peers. Completing market research and allowing tastings of my goodies at the school allowed me access to what my peers would essentially purchase from me. It was GENIUS!

BAKEOLOGY

SCIENCE - TECHNOLOGY - ENGINEERING - ARTS - MATHEMATICS

YEAST: A LEAVENING AGENT

S.T.E.A.M EXPERIMENT: ELEPHANT TOOTHPASTE

With this experiment...
You'll use chemistry and some of your baking skills to create elephant toothpaste. This reaction releases heat, fizz, and a lot of oozing foam. Get your gloves, grab some strong hydrogen peroxide, and get ready to release a mega-sized tower of chemistry!!!

MATERIALS NEEDED...
SALON-STRENGTH HYDROGEN PEROXIDE (6%)
TALL GLASS JAR OR VASE
FOOD COLORING
SPOON

DISH SPOON
WATER
SMALL CUP
1 PACKAGE OF ACTIVE DRY YEAST
LARGE METAL BAKING TRAY
MEASURING CUP
RUBBER GLOVES

PROCEDURE

Safety note: hydrogen peroxide can irritate your skin when touched! Make sure you use your gloves when conducting experiment! Never drink hydrogen peroxide!

1. Pour ½ cup of salon-strength hydrogen peroxide into a tall vase
2. Add 10 drops of food coloring to the hydrogen peroxide in the vase, then stir to thoroughly pour color your peroxide.
3. Add 1-2 tablespoons of dish soap to the vase and swirl it around to combine the mixture.
4. Pour 4 tablespoons of warm water into your small cup. Add the packet of yeast and slowly stir the yeast into the water. Let it sit for a couple of minutes until it looks foamy and starts to give a bready smell.
5. Put the vase in the center of your baking tray. Then, dump the yeast into the vase and stand back!
6. After your foaming explosion is done feel the sides of the vase. Is it warm? You've just created an exothermic (heat) reaction with your fizzing, oozing, dose of chemistry!

What's Happening?

Hydrogen peroxide molecules consist of two hydrogen atoms and two oxygen atoms. When the peroxide is introduced to yeast, the yeast acts quickly breaking apart the oxygen from the hydrogen. In baking the yeast is used as a leavening agent which allows the cake to raise or not raise as it reacts with sugar to create carbon dioxide gas and alcohol. The alcohol evaporates as the dough/cake bakes and the carbon dioxide gas bubbles causes the dough/cake to rise!

Math and Measurement

How do we make math fun for kids? We give kids real-life objects or experiences with math to develop their skills in a super fun or even YUMMY way! Math is one of the easiest subjects to use if you would like to "cook things up a notch". Measurement is the act of finding the size or amount of something in number form. We can measure length, how far from one end to another. We can measure area, which is the inside dimensions of a flat surface on all sides. Volume or capacity which the amount of space that is filled or occupied. To see how much matter something contains, you would find mass or weight. The temperature is how hot or cold someone or something is, usually on the Fahrenheit of Celsius scale. Last but not least, there is Time. We measure time in so many areas of our lives. From the time we wake up until the time we lay down to rest. But most importantly we are responsible for managing our time when we bake. Making sure all of our baked goods are baking the right amount of time to produce a beautifully delicious product. We also measure the time we spend baking when we are calculating our service fees. When running a baking business, you want to always get paid for your skills and time. Just as real money has help me to understand how money works, how to budget better, and how to create wealth in my life, it has also enhanced my knowledge in the following areas due to measurement: understanding fractions, division, multiplication, subtraction, addition, percentages, and probability.

There are two different systems that are used to measure:

Metric System

United States Standard Units

Define the measurement systems and list the units of measurement here:

_____

_____

_____

RECIPE: Rainbow Layered Dream Cake Jars

PREP TIME: 45 minutes
BAKE TIME: 20 minutes
TOTAL TIME: 1 hour 5 minutes

TOOLS YOU NEED:
6-4 oz. mason jars, cake pans, mixer, mixing bowl, spatula, ice cream scooper, 6 small mixing bowls, food coloring (red, yellow, blue, green)

INGREDIENTS YOU NEED:
1 cup unsalted butter, softened
3 eggs
1 cup buttermilk
¼ cup heavy whipping cream
2 ½ cups white granulated sugar
3 cups all-purpose flour
½ teaspoon salt
¼ heavy whipping cream
1 teaspoon baking soda
Food coloring: red, yellow, blue, green
FROSTING: It's your choice but we love American Buttercream!

INSTRUCTIONS:

1. Preheat oven to 325 F. Generously grease and flour 6 (9-inch cake pans.) If you use 6-inch pans you can make cupcakes with the leftover batter!

2. Combine flour, baking powder, and salt in a bowl using your whisk and sit to the side.

3. In a large bowl cream together, sugar and butter. Mix in eggs until thoroughly incorporated. Then mix in vanilla extract, buttermilk and heavy cream.

4. Mix in half of dry ingredients (flour mixture) into wet ingredients (sugar mixture). When mixture is combined, mix in the rest of the dry ingredients.

5. Divide the batter into six bowls (about 1 cup of batter per bowl batter per bowl. 12. Add food coloring to each bowl to create a vibrant red, orange, yellow, green, blue, and violet. (see note on how to make colors) Pour each colored batter into the prepared pans and spread out into an even layer. (layers will be thin)

6. Bake for 10-15 minutes or until center is set. Do not overbake. Remove from oven and let cakes cool in the pan until pans are warm enough to touch. Run a spatula around the edges of the pans to loosen the cake and then very carefully remove the cakes from the pans. Place on a cooling rack and cool completely.

7. Now this will be fun!!! Take you me hand and crumble about 1/2 cup of cake in your hand starting with the purple layer. Place in your mason jar. Followed by the blue, crumble in the same amount in the same jar to create layers. Follow the same procedure to create every layer. Followed by crumbled green layer, yellow layer, orange layer and finally the red layer. Create multiple jars just like this or switch the colors to add uniqueness to every jar. Once every layer and jar is complete it's time to frost. Choose your favorite icing! Now add frosting to the top of last layer. Don't forget to add sprinkles! Stick a spoon in it and enjoy! Left overs can be sealed with the mason jar cap and placed in the refrigerator or freezer for longer storage.

Note Colors: Be sure to add in enough food coloring to the batter to make the colors very vibrant. To make orange, create a vibrant yellow and then add drops of red until you have orange. To make violet make a vibrant red and add drops of blue.

BAKEOLOGY CONNECT!

SHERKENNA BUGGS CHEF KENNA

Let me share with you a little bit about an amazing mentor of mine. Having a passion for food, a love for cooking, and an eye for creativity is where her culinary journey began. When she was 16 years old, close to my age, she met Ryan Luttrell. Ryan Luttrell is a professional chef, amongst other amazing things. In his career as a chef and pastry chef, he has held roles in New York, Phoenix, Memphis, Los Angeles, and San Francisco and has worked as a food stylist for the Food Network. We were coincidently from the same hometown of Grand Junction, TN. Ryan soon became a friend and a mentor to Sherkenna. He inspired Sherkenna to follow my dreams. He opened her eyes to what the culinary world had to offer and to the opportunities that could soon arise. Who knew those opportunities would happen so soon after meeting Ryan.

In the year 2012, Sherkenna ventured out as an entrepreneur and started her business Chef Kenna. Chef Kenna is a local business that provides private culinary experiences for looking for a whole lot of Memphis flare. Chef Kenna attended L'Ecole Culinaire in Memphis, where she developed her culinary skills as well as her brand. She credits her success to L'Ecole's more intimate learning environment, which gave her more instructional time with her professor to become the expert she is today.

Chef Kenna is located in Fayette-Ware Vocational CTE Building. Chef Kenna specializes in serving her delicious pasta and seafood dishes to thousands to date. She has also earned her seat as a celebrity pastry chef for her amazing custom desserts. Most importantly Chef Kenna sows back into the lives of other aspiring and professional chefs. She encourages, supports, and offers her expertise in ways that demonstrate her will to give back in such a phenomenal way. She is an advocate for young chefs and black chefs across the globe. You can see Chef Kenna on Hell's Kitchen Season 15 and follow her on Instagram and Facebook @ChefKenna.

I truly appreciate you in my life Chef Kenna! Baked in love, Chef Ashalah Michelle

Homemade Gelato With Fresh Strawberry Compote

Ingredients
- 1c sugar
- 4c heavy cream
- 1/4c light corn syrup
- 1/2c warm water
- 2T raspberry sweet fruit vinegar
- 2 pints strawberries, hulled and halved lengthwise.

Gelato Instructions

1. Combine 1/2c sugar, cream, and corn syrup in small saucepan over low heat and cook stirring occasionally, for 2-3 min or til sugar is completely dissolved.
2. Remove from heat and let cool to room temperature.
3. Transfer the cooled mixture to an ice cream machine. Transfer gelato into airtight container and place in freezer until serving.

Compote and Toppings Instructions

1. Heat the remaining 1/2c sugar in a small, heavy saucepan over medium heat.
2. When it melts and turn golden brown, gradually stir in the water and vinegar. Simmer for about 5 mins.
3. Remove from heat and cool to room temperature.
4. Put the strawberries in a bowl and pour the cool syrup over the top and let marinate at room temp for 1 hour.
5. Put scoops of gelato in a bowl and top with the berries and a mint.

Caramel Apple Cheesecake

Ingredients

Crust:
- 2 cups all-purpose flour
- 1/2 cup firmly packed brown sugar
- 1 cup (2 sticks) butter, softened

Cheesecake Filling:
- 3 (8-ounce) packages cream cheese, softened
- 3/4 cup sugar, plus 2 tablespoons, divided
- 3 large eggs
- 1 1/2 teaspoons vanilla extract

Apples:
- 3 Granny Smith apples, peeled, cored and finely chopped
- 1/2 teaspoon ground cinnamon
- 1/4 teaspoon ground nutmeg

Streusel Topping:
- 1 cup firmly packed brown sugar
- 1 cup all-purpose flour
- 1/2 cup quick cooking oats
- 1/2 cup (1 stick) butter, softened

PREP TIME: 1 HOUR
BAKE TIME: 40-60 minutes or until filling set

INSTRUCTIONS

1. Preheat oven to 350 degrees F.
2. In a medium bowl, combine flour and brown sugar.
3. Cut in butter with a pastry blender (or 2 forks) until mixture is crumbly.
4. Press evenly into a 9×13 baking pan lined with heavy-duty aluminum foil. Bake 15 minutes or until lightly browned.
5. In a large bowl, beat cream cheese with 3/4 cup sugar in an electric mixer at medium speed until smooth.
6. Then add eggs, 1 at a time, and vanilla. Stir to combine. Pour over warm crust.
7. In a small bowl, stir together chopped apples, remaining 2 tablespoons sugar, cinnamon, and nutmeg. Spoon evenly over cream cheese mixture.
8. Sprinkle evenly with Streusel topping.
9. Bake 40-45 minutes, or until filling is set.
10. Drizzle with caramel topping and let cool. Serve cold and enjoy!

CHEF JJ MASTERMIND
KIRKGATE KITCHEN

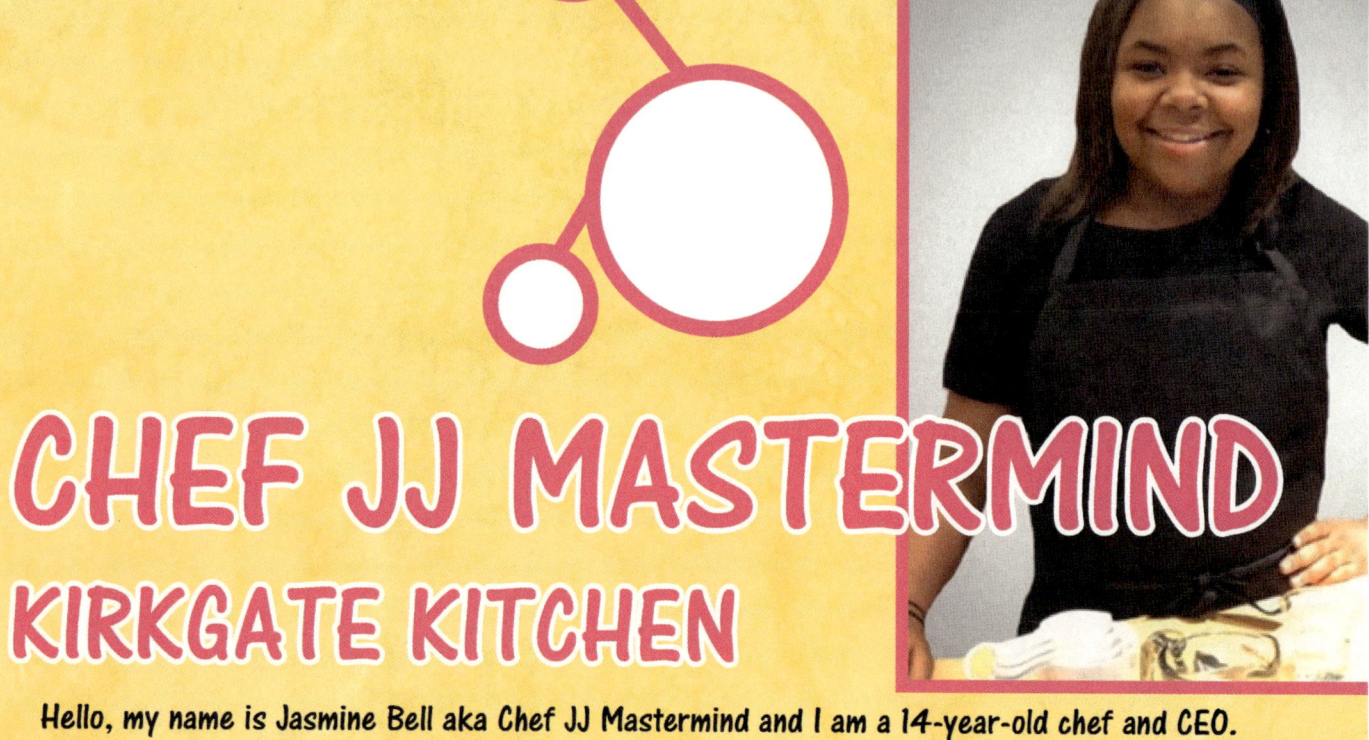

Hello, my name is Jasmine Bell aka Chef JJ Mastermind and I am a 14-year-old chef and CEO. Kirkgate Kitchen, my catering, sweet treat, and custom culinary apparel business was born out of my desire to be a World-Renowned Chef and Culinary Entrepreneur. I started cooking at an early age with my mom, grandmother, and aunt. During the Summer of 2015, I attended a local STEAM Summer Camp that featured academics and career clubs. It was there my true passion for the culinary world was ignited. Exploring cuisines from around the world made me want to learn more. So, I researched and participated in local cooking classes for kids. After posting a few photos of my plates on social media, my aunt contacted my parents about auditioning for MasterChef Junior. I was a little hesitant but decided I wanted to step up to the challenge. After the initial auditions, I was invited to Los Angeles, CA to audition for a Top 40 spot. When it was all said and done, I became a MasterChef Junior contestant and appeared as "Jazzy" on Season 5. It was an honor to be the first NC representative on MasterChef and have Gordon Ramsey and Christina Tosi taste my food.

As a result, I came home and continued to fuel my passion. During one of my culinary classes, I met Chef Clark Barlowe, the owner of the Heirloom restaurant and he invited me to stage in his restaurant. We collaborated a 5 Course tasting dinner in May of 2017. As I continued my journey, I had the unique opportunity to meet Carla Hall when she invited me to be a guest on, "The Chew". We, along with the other hosts made Sweet Potato Poppers. Most recently, I competed on the Emmy nominated show, Top Chef Jr. which aired on Universal Kids. I, along with 11 other very talented young chefs, I cooked for renowned chef and celebrities. I advanced to top 5 on the show and walked away with experiences that will last a lifetime. In an effort to promote the inaugural season of Top Chef Jr., I was able to team up with another Jr. Chef on The Today Show, in NY. June 2018, Chef Clark allowed me and Katelyn R. from Top Chef to collaborate and take over his restaurant to serve a 6 Course Tasting Menu. Nowadays, I still stage at Heirloom, experimenting in the kitchen, and making guest appearances on local TV stations. Additionally, I am taking a culinary course at my high school which will allow me to increase my skills.

Chocolate Dipped Cream Puffs Filled With an Orange Whipped Cream and a Raspberry Coulis

Tools Needed
- Non-stick pot
- Wooden spoon
- Saucepan
- Mesh Colander
- Sheet Tray
- Parchment Paper
- Piping Bag or Ziploc Bag
- Zester
- Whisk
- 2 medium bowls

Ingredients

Cream Puffs
- 1 cup of water
- 1 stick (½ cup) of butter
- 1 ¼ cup of flour
- 5 eggs

Raspberry Coulis
- 6 oz Raspberry Pack
- ¼ cup of granulated sugar

Whipped Cream
1 cup of heavy whipping cream
¼ cup of powdered sugar
1 tablespoon of orange zest

Chocolate Ganache
8 oz of chocolate chips
1 cup of heavy cream

PREP TIME: 10 MINUTES
TOTAL TIME: 45 minutes

Directions

Cream Puffs

1. Get a non-stick pot and bring the water, sugar, butter, and salt to a boil.
2. Sift flour. Add the flour and stir with a wooden spoon until the dough forms into a ball on high heat.
3. Take the dough and add into a mixer using the paddle attachment. Mix on a low speed for about 30 seconds. This allows the dough to cool down a bit.
4. Now turning it up to a medium speed add in the eggs one at a time. Let the eggs get mixed in the batter before adding in the next one.
5. While still warm add the batter to a piping bag. Pipe the batter onto a parchment lined sheet pan creating small circles. Let each circle be about 1 inch apart.
6. Before putting it in the oven, dab your finger in some and rub water on the top of each circle. This will help the top of the cream puffs not to burn.
7. Bake at 400 degrees Fahrenheit for 25-30 minutes until golden brown.

While the cream puffs are baking you can make the whipped cream, raspberry coulis, and chocolate ganache.

Raspberry Coulis

1. In a saucepan add the sugar and raspberries. Bring to a boil.
2. On medium heat let the sugar dissolve.
3. Strain out the seeds by using a fine mesh colander in a bowl.
4. Put the bowl in the fridge to cool

Orange Whipped Cream

1. Zest 1 tablespoon of an orange.
2. In a bowl add a mix together the zest, heavy cream, and powdered sugar. Mix until you form medium to stiff peaks.

Chocolate Ganache

1. Using a double boiler (a pot of simmering water and a glass bowl added on top) add the chocolate and cream into the bowl. Stir constantly until smooth.

Before assembling let the cream puffs sit and cool. Now to put it all together, dip the top of the cream puffs in the chocolate. Let the chocolate harden on top. Once harden, cut the cream puffs in half. Add a scoop of whipped cream and pour some coulis on top of the whipped cream to the bottom half. Add the cream puff top and you can garnish with powdered sugar.

S.T.E.A.M CONNECTION:

S.T.E.A.M is connected to my recipe because I am critically thinking about how to properly measure ingredients, use the correct temperature to achieve a perfect product, and I used creativity to craft this recipe. Throughout making the dish, I am able to apply science, art, math, and technology together to make sure I execute each aspect correctly to get a delicious finished product. Not only did I use it in this recipe, but I use it on a day to day basis. STEAM is a part of my lifestyle. Every day I face problems that need solving and with each problem I use STEAM. STEAM helps solve problems by teaching us different ways to investigate the problem, to approach the situation with different ways to solve it, and how to come to productive solutions.

FOLLOW CHEF JJ's Journey

Instagram- @chefjjmastermind
Twitter- @chefjasminebell
Website- kirkgatekitchen.weebly.com

CHEF LAURYN
LALA'S SUGAR & SPICE

Lauryn Strong, known as Chef LaLa, is a 16-year-old entrepreneur that has her own catering company known as Lala's Sugar & Spice. She has been baking since she was 6 years old and started her company in 2016. She was introduced in the food industry by her mentor Tregaye Frazier who is Food Network Star season 12 winner and winner of Guy's Grocery Games. She was the 2017 Junior Atlanta's Trailblazer Awards recipient. Lala loves making creative cupcakes that bring flavor and life to the pallet such as her delicious Maple Bourbon Cupcakes, Chicken and waffles Cupcakes; Berry Berry, Chocolate Oreo, Strawberry filled Cupcakes and much more. She has won multiple junior competitions and has been a vendor at the Atlanta Ice Cream Festival for two years in a row. Chef Lala has also been honored to help provide service in the Chef of the Worlds event for two years in a row.

Easy No Bake Vegan Sweet Potato Cheesecake

Tools Needed
- food processor
- 2 bowls
- nonstick springform pan
- spatula
- aluminum foil
- plastic wrap

Ingredients

Crust
- 2/3 cup pecans
- 1/3 cup walnuts
- 6 Medjool dates pitted
- 1/4 cup unsweetened coconut flakes
- pinch sea salt

Filling:
- 2 cups raw cashews soaked in boiling water for 1 1/2 hours
- 2/3 cup pure maple syrup or honey
- 1/2 cup canned coconut milk
- 1/4 teaspoon salt
- 2 1/2 tablespoons coconut oil at room temperature
- 3 tablespoons lemon juice

Topping:
- 3 cooked sweet potatoes
- 3 tablespoons of maple syrup
- 1 teaspoon of vanilla

PREP TIME: 10 minutes
TOTAL TIME: 3-4 HOURS CHILL

Directions

Be sure to bring all of your filling ingredients to room temperature before you begin. Otherwise, your filling will not be smooth!

INSTRUCTIONS

1. Add cashews to a bowl and cover with boiling hot water. Let set, uncovered, for 1 1/2 hours. Rinse and drain thoroughly.
2. Combine the nuts in a food processor and pulse until you get a coarse mixture. Add the rest of the crust ingredients and pulse several times until it starts clumping up and forming together.
3. Transfer the crust mixture into a 6" or 7" nonstick springform pan. Press down with your fingers to pack it evenly into the bottom of the pan. If it starts to get sticky, lightly wet your fingers with warm water. Set aside.
4. Add drained cashews and the rest of the filling ingredients to the bowl of your food processor or into a high-speed blender pitcher.
5. Blend until creamy and smooth. Scape down the sides as needed. *Taste and adjust accordingly. Be sure to add more lemon juice if it's too sweet, more maple syrup if it isn't sweet enough, or a pinch more of salt for more balance!*
6. Pour the filling over the crust evenly. Tap on the counter a couple of times to release any air bubbles that may have formed. Set aside.
7. Combine the sweet potatoes, maple syrup, and vanilla in the bowl of a food processor until pulverized. Add this mixture on top of the filling.
8. Add this mixture on top of the filling.
9. Cover lightly with plastic wrap and seal the top with aluminum foil. Let it set in the freezer for at least 4-6 hours or overnight.
10. When you are ready to serve, pull out the cheesecake and allow it to sit at room temperature for about 10-15 minutes before serving.
11. Enjoy!

S.T.E.A.M CONNECTION

S.T.E.A.M is infused with my everyday life as well as baking. When I bake, I use measurements, mixtures, and compounds to create cuisines that explode on the pallet. There are many appliances that are available for baking. I research to find the best suited for my recipes. I use the mixer to combine my ingredients and create the perfect cupcake. Engineering is evident in the way in which I create a dish from start to finish. I plan each intricate piece to ensure the dish comes together to provide the perfect combination. Also, the art of my product is displayed in the creativity I use to make the product appealing visually, such as using decorative designs on my product. Baking takes precision and specific techniques in order to ensure that my product is great quality. I predict the outcome based on a recipe. My process is the dependent variable and the observation is the taste test.

AYONNAH TINSLEY
YAYASTARS.COM

Ayonnah Tinsley is a 15-year-old entrepreneur and aspiring aeronautical engineer who owns a travel blog, and it all started with a little green notebook. Since she was seven years old, she was reviewing everything in sight. A year later Tinsley turned this all into a website, YaYaStars.com. She has been featured in Huffington Post, Good Morning Washington, and more! When she is not trying a new restaurant, teaching students about STEM, or zipping through an airport, the teen CEO enjoys volunteering, participating in student government, and running varsity track and field for her high school.

S.T.E.A.M CONNECTION

What does an airplane, cookie and a laptop --- have in common? These are all things that helped me start my own company when I was eight years old! I combined my love of travel, food, and STEM into my own company YaYaStars.com so I could share my passion with the world. As an only child, I often find interesting ways to keep myself entertained. One way was by deciding to be a food critic when I was seven years old. I took my favorite notebook everywhere I went and jotted down my reviews of restaurants, movies and fun places I would travel with my parents. I would rate the experience with stars based on if the food and service were exceptional. When I was eight, I discovered that my friend and I both traveled to the Blue Ridge Mountains over the summer, and I wanted to be able to share the experience beyond my notebook so other kids could review and share their favorite places to travel, too. And that's how YaYaStars.com was born. I discovered creating my own website would let me share my reviews with kids all over the world! And it has helped me meet so many great Kidpreneurs and STEM advocates (like Chef Ashalah).

A perk of having my own review blog for kids is that companies send me their products and I provide an honest review. 'Cook Me Up A Notch' is such an amazing company and not only is the owner a teenager, but she is one of the nicest Internet friends. Chef Ashalah sent me a batch of her yummy vegan cookies. Yeah, I know. "It can't be good if it was vegan!" However, have you ever tried vegan desserts? If you had a bad experience you have to order a dozen of Chef Ashalah's vegan cookies for a new perspective! I was so excited to receive these cookies and another reason to buy from Chef Ashalah is her packaging! Seriously, it is so professional and cute and completely goals - and most importantly no cookies were damaged or crumbled from their long journey. The cookies were delicious, and I highly recommend you try them or any of her tasty treats!

I know you are wondering, so where does the airplane come in? It was also during this time that I took my first trip to the Smithsonian Air and Space Museum and discovered my love for aeronautics. I decided that I would like to be an aeronautical engineer when I grow up and I've been involved with STEM ever since. I love mentoring kids and teaching them about STEM topics. I also use STEM for my website since I code it and create the graphics myself. I often volunteer to teach kids about STEM to encourage more kids of color and especially girls to pursue STEM careers. In addition, I get to travel often and being on a plane is one of my favorite adventures. I get to chat with the pilots and impress them with my knowledge.

And there you have it - my story of how an airplane, cookies, and a laptop led me to my STEM journey. Visit me @yayastars on all social media to keep up with my adventures!

Peace & Travel,

Ayonnah

Pictured: Ashalah's Vegan Chocolate Chip Cookie Ice Cream Sandwich

Ronnie Thomas

Ronnie Thomas applies his 19 years of STEM teaching experience to ensure that all learners are challenged. He is an enthusiastic and passionate technology educator with a solid commitment to the social, academic and developmental growth of every student. Known for his engaging and versatile teaching methods, Thomas has the ability to inspire hands-on learning experiences that capture a student's imagination. Founder of Georgia Science & Robotics Academy, Inc 501c3 and Fun Weird Science, LLC, Ronnie resides in Atlanta with his wife and three children.

Fun Weird Science Offerings

Online STEM Courses, Monthly Science Kits, Saturday/Summer Camps, Science Shows, Birthday Parties, In-school field trips

Check out this cool experiment provided by FUN WEIRD SCIENCE that uses sugar crystals to create a tasty treat for you to enjoy!

Make Rock Candy at Home

- Granulated Cane sugar (Try Imperial Sugar or Dixie Crystals for better results.)
- Water
- Large glass container (microwave-safe)
- Smaller glass jar
- Measuring cups
- Heavy stirring spoon
- Pencil
- Food coloring
- String (new preferred)
- Scissors
- Wax paper (or parchment)
- Adult supervision

1. Pour 3 cups of sugar into the large glass container
2. Add 1 cup of water to the sugar. Stir the water (a solvent) and sugar (a solute) together with a heavy spoon. The solution will be very viscous (thick) because there is more sugar than water so stir very well.
3. With the help of an adult, place the sugar and water solution into the microwave for 2:00 minutes on high. Remove from microwave and stir, then heat for an additional 2:00. You can also put in a pot and bring to boil on top of the stove.
4. Have an adult to remove the hot solution and stir. The solution is less viscous (runnier) than before you heated it.
5. Add 4-8 drops of food coloring to the solution and stir thoroughly.
6. Pour colored solution into a smaller container.
7. Wrap a piece of new string around the middle of a pencil that is longer than the container is tall. Lay the pencil over the top of the container and let the string hang over the container on the outside (do not let the string get wet). Trim the string so that it is 2/3 the height of the container. The string needs to be shorter than the container.
8. Lower the string into the solution and let it soak up the colored solution for a short time. Lay the pencil and soaked string on a piece of wax paper so the string is perpendicular to the pencil (it should look like capital letter T)
9. Let the solution cool to room temperature and the string dry completely.
10. Place the string into the solution (you may have to apply some pressure because the solution will become more viscous as it cools). Let the string sit inside solution for a week. You can lay a paper towel over the container to keep out dust and bugs.

Great Grammie, Baby Me, & Grammie

Grammie & I after pressing my hair

Amari and I headed to church with Grammie

Lessons from my Grammie's Kitchen
By: Chef Ashalah Michelle

The last section of this book is dedicated to my grandmother. I called her Grammie. Her real name was Alycia Michelle Wright. We shared the same initials "AMW" and the same love for helping others! She helped me realize that baking may not always come with the perfect recipe or measurement, but it's made up of a whole lot of love. My Grammie showed me how to carry the love out of my hands into whatever you mixed, kneaded, or stirred. My Grammie introduced me to baking one Sunday morning while she prepared biscuits for the family. At the time, my grandmother lived with myself, my mom, and my brother. She would show me step by step how to make biscuits, a recipe passed down in our family. She would say first, get a nice wide bowl big enough to spread your flour around it.

Pour flour around the inside of the bowl, depending on how many biscuits you want to make. You can see already there are no real measurements or not a recipe in sight. Then she would say, get your Crisco and place a lump of it in the center (this also based on how many biscuits you were making). So, for a family of 4, I would say to put at least 2 large mixing spoons of Crisco (lard) in the middle. Thirdly, make sure the flour is pushed to the side, you do not want it to touch the Crisco yet. Pour buttermilk over the Crisco until it almost covers it. Using your hand, work in (knead or mesh together) Crisco and buttermilk until the mixer has come to a smoother consistency. Once the Crisco and buttermilk are combined, slowly add in the flour little by little. While turning the bowl, put a little flour into the Crisco and buttermilk mixture forming a ball. Continue to do that until the ball becomes smooth and round. Put a little flour on your hands so that the dough doesn't stick. Pull out small sections of your ball of dough and make a small ball. Then press it down in a greased pan. After about 30 minutes in the oven, you will have some delicious buttermilk biscuits. While hot, Grammie would rub butter on the top and cover the biscuits with a towel to keep them from hardening. Sometimes I will eat them with strawberry jam or maple syrup but other times they were good just the way they were.

See, my grandma taught me almost everything by her actions. She would show you and she expected you to learn. She taught me that you always keep your kitchen clean as you go. Never leave your counters filled with the mess from food prep or with dirty dishes. As biscuits are baking and salmon croquettes are frying, go ahead and wash the dishes she would say. She would always make cheese grits and eggs with the biscuits and salmon. We would wake up from our slumber to the smell of homemade biscuits. As Grammie got older, she couldn't make biscuits as easily as she once did. This is when she started showing me how to do it. Mine is still not as perfect as Grammie's but it sure is fun making them because I feel closer to her when I do.
I found this sweet video on Youtube and it's not my Grammie but she makes biscuits just like my Grammie. Check it out https://youtu.be/BoKHoOlXmQg, You're going to love it!

Glossary

A

A physical change- in a substance doesn't change what the substance is. In a chemical change where there is a chemical reaction, a new substance is formed and energy is either given off or absorbed. For example, if a piece of paper is cut up into small pieces it still is paper.

Absorbent - a substance that can soak up a liquid, or to take in energy and retain it.

Absorber - an absorber does not reflect or transmit particles or radiation that hit it. Aluminium foil is an absorber of alpha particles. A dark, dull surface is an absorber of infra-red radiation.

B

Bake: To cook food in an oven, surrounded with dry heat; also called baking.

Batter: An uncooked pourable mixture usually made up
of flour, water or milk, possibly even butter or eggs depending on the recipe.

Beat - To mix together, creaming. To aerate by beating.

Beat: To stir rapidly to make a mixture smooth, using a whisk, spoon, or mixer.
Blanch: To cook briefly in boiling water to seal in flavor and color.
Blend: To blend ingredients is to mix two or more of them together with a mixer, spoon, or by hand.
Boil: To cook in bubbling water that has reached 212 degrees Fahrenheit.
Bone: To remove bones from poultry, meat, or fish.
Braise: To cook first by browning, then gently simmering in a pan.
Bread: To coat with crumbs or cornmeal before cooking.
Broil: To cook on a rack or grill under or over direct heat, usually in oven.
Brown: To cook over high heat, usually on top of the stove; to brown in the oven under a broiler.

C

Caramelize: To heat sugar until it liquefies and becomes a syrup ranging in color from golden to dark brown.
Chemical Reaction: a process that involves rearrangement of the molecular or ionic structure of a substance, as opposed to a change in physical form or a nuclear reaction.
Chemical Leavener: combination of baking soda, an acid such as
cream of tartar, and a starch such as cornstarch.
Combine: To combine ingredients is to mix them together until they are evenly distributed or mixture is smooth.
Consistence - a degree of thickness or smoothness of a substance.

Glossary

Controlled Variable - the things that you try to keep the same in an experiment or investigation.

Core: To remove the seeds or tough woody centers from fruits and vegetables.

Cream: The butterfat portion of milk. Also, to beat ingredients, usually sugar and a fat, until smooth and fluffy.

Cube: To cut food into small (about 1/2- inch) cubes.

Current - is a flow of electric charge. The current is a metallic conductor is due to a flow of negatively charged electrons.

Cut in: To distribute a solid fat in flour using a cutting motion, with 2 knives used scissors-fashion or a pastry blender, until divided evenly into tiny pieces. Usually refers to making pastry.

D

Data - a collection of observations, measurements and/or facts.

Decompose - the breaking down of parts from a whole - to decay or rot, wasting away.

Deep-fry: To cook by completely immersing food in hot fat.

Dense - made up of very closely packed particles.

Dilute - is to make a liquid weaker or thinner by adding more liquid, usually more water.

Dispersion - is the splitting of white light into the seven colors of the visible spectrum - rainbow.

Dissolving - is the process that occurs when a solute is added to a solvent and the solute disappears. The particles of the solute fit between the particles of the solvent. The solute can be recovered by the evaporation process. To mix a solid with a liquid so it becomes a liquid as well. To melt, to become a liquid (ice melting, sugar dissolving in hot tea).

Distillation - this is to separate a liquid from other liquids by boiling it and condensing the steam. A substance that has been through an evaporation and condensing process.

Dust: To coat lightly with confectioners' sugar or cocoa.

E

Endothermic process-An endothermic process is any process which requires or absorbs energy from its surroundings, usually in the form of heat.

Erode - is to wear away.

Erosion - is the process where rocks are worn away.

Evaluating - to decide if you have done something the best way and seeing what you could improve.

Evaporation - is the process in which a liquid changes to a vapour, due to particles leaving the surface of the liquid. A liquid turns to a gas. Changing from a liquid or a solid into vapours (gas).

Evidence - is anything that gives a reason to believe something.

Exothermic reaction-An exothermic reaction is a chemical reaction that releases energy through light or heat.

Glossary

Exothermic reaction- An exothermic reaction is a chemical reaction that releases energy through light or heat.
Expand - is when the size of a substance increases due to being heated. The particles gain energy and move further apart.
Experiment - a test to find something out.
Explosion - is a very rapid reaction accompanied by a large expansion in gases.

F

fats like butter, margarine, or shortening together with a mixer, large spoon,
Fillet: A flat piece of boneless meat, poultry, or fish. Also, to cut

flour (moisture absorber). Most common type is double-acting baking powder,
Fold- Part of the layering process in the making of puff pastry.
Fondant- Used as a decorative coating and as an addition to butter creams. Made from boiled sugar, water and glucose.
Food Hygiene - Making sure that food is handled, stored, prepared and served so as not to allow the food to be contaminated.

Food poisoning- The result of bad food hygiene leading to sickness and diarrhoea and sometimes death.
Force - is a push or pull. Force is measured in units called newtons (N).
Formula - is a way of writing scientific information using letters, numbers and signs.
Freeze - is when you cool something to a very low temperature and it usually forms ice.
Friction - occurs when two surfaces move over each other. Air resistance and water resistance are friction forces caused by the movement of something through the air or the water.
Function - is the special purpose or use of something.

G

Ganache- A mixture of fresh dairy cream and melted chocolate.
Gas - is a state of matter in which the particles move rapidly and are very spread out.
Glaze: To coat foods with glossy mixtures such as
Grill: To cook food on a rack under or over direct heat, as on a barbecue or in a broiler.

I

Incorporate- Blend and combine ingredients together.
Infuse- Soak in a liquid to extract the flavour.

Ingredients: any of the foods or substances that are combined to make a particular dish.

Glossary

K

Kinetic Energy - is the kind of energy in moving things.
Knead: To blend dough together with hands or in a mixer to form a finished product.

M

Marble: To partly mix two colors of cake batter or icing so that the colors are in decorative swirls.
Marinate: To soak in a flavored liquid; usually refers
Mixture - is two or more substances mixed together without actually joining them so that they can be separated again.
Molecule - is a group of atoms joined together.

N

Nonperishable - able to be stored for a long time without spoiling nonperishable food items such a canned foods or cereal.

O

Ology- the science or branch of knowledge

P

Particles - are the extremely tiny parts (substances) that scientists believe everything is made up of.

Perishable - Food that is perishable has to be used quickly or it will decay. These foods should be placed in the refrigerator to remain fresh a longer period of time.

Petit Four: A delicate cake or pastry small enough to be eaten in one or two bites.

Predicting - to say what you think is going to happen in an experiment or investigation.
Preheat — To preheat an oven is to heat an empty oven
Purée: To mash or grind food until completely smooth, usually in a processor.

R

Reaction - is something that happens in response to something else.
Reaction Time - is the time that elapses between an event occurring and aperson responding to the event.
Recycled - is when something is used again in a system.
Reflect - is to bounce something back from a surface.
Reflection - is the change in direction when light or other wave motion rebounds at a boundary between two materials.

Glossary

Refraction - is the change in speed when light or other wave motions passes from one material into another. The change in speed causes a change in wavelength and may cause a change in direction.

Reliable - things that can be taken to be true.

Research - is an investigation or study to find out facts in order to reach a conclusion.

Residue - is something that remains behind or is left over.

Result - is what happens at the end of an experiment.

S

Scientific method- Step 1: Ask a question. For the first step, help your child form a question, hopefully one that can be answered! ...Step 2: Do background research. ...Step 3: Construct a hypothesis. ...Step 4: Test your hypothesis by doing an experiment. ...Step 5: Analyze the data and draw a conclusion. ...Step 6: Share your results.

Simmer: To cook in liquid just below the boiling.

Solution - chemical: is the mixture of two or more substances, a solute dissolves in a solvent. The substance made when a solid disappears in a liquid. The process of solving a problem.

Streusel (straysel): A crumbly topping for baked

goods, consisting of fat, sugar, and flour rubbed together.

T

Temperature - is a measure of how hot or cold an object is.
Texture - is the appearance, feel and structure of a substance.
Thermometer - is an instrument used to measure temperature.

V

Variables - are the things that can change during an experiment. Something that can vary during an experiment.
Vegetables - a plant or part of a plant used as food, typically as accompaniment to meat or fish, such as a cabbage, potato, carrot, or bean.
Vertebrates - are animals with a backbone.
Volume - is how much room something takes up. It is measured in centimeters (cm3).

W

Wash- with Egg...Milk... Water... used as a pre-bake, usually by brush, or
as a post bake using icing or a glaze.

Whip: To beat food with a whisk or mixer to whipping with a spoon, electric mixture, wire whisk, or beater to create a fluffy substance.

Whisk: To beat with a fork or whisk to mix, blend, or incorporate air.

Z

Zest: The outer layer of fruit shredded to make tiny pieces.

Glossary adopted from various different online sources such as goodhousekeeping.com, webster.com, and shrinkingkitchen.com

STAY CONNECTED WITH US!

Cook Me Up A Notch:
Cookies, Cakes, and Culinary Creations

---

website: www.cookmeupanotch.com
social media platforms: @cookmeupanotch

Speaking Engagements
Baked Goods
Baking Classes
Birthday Parties
Bakeology 101 Workshops

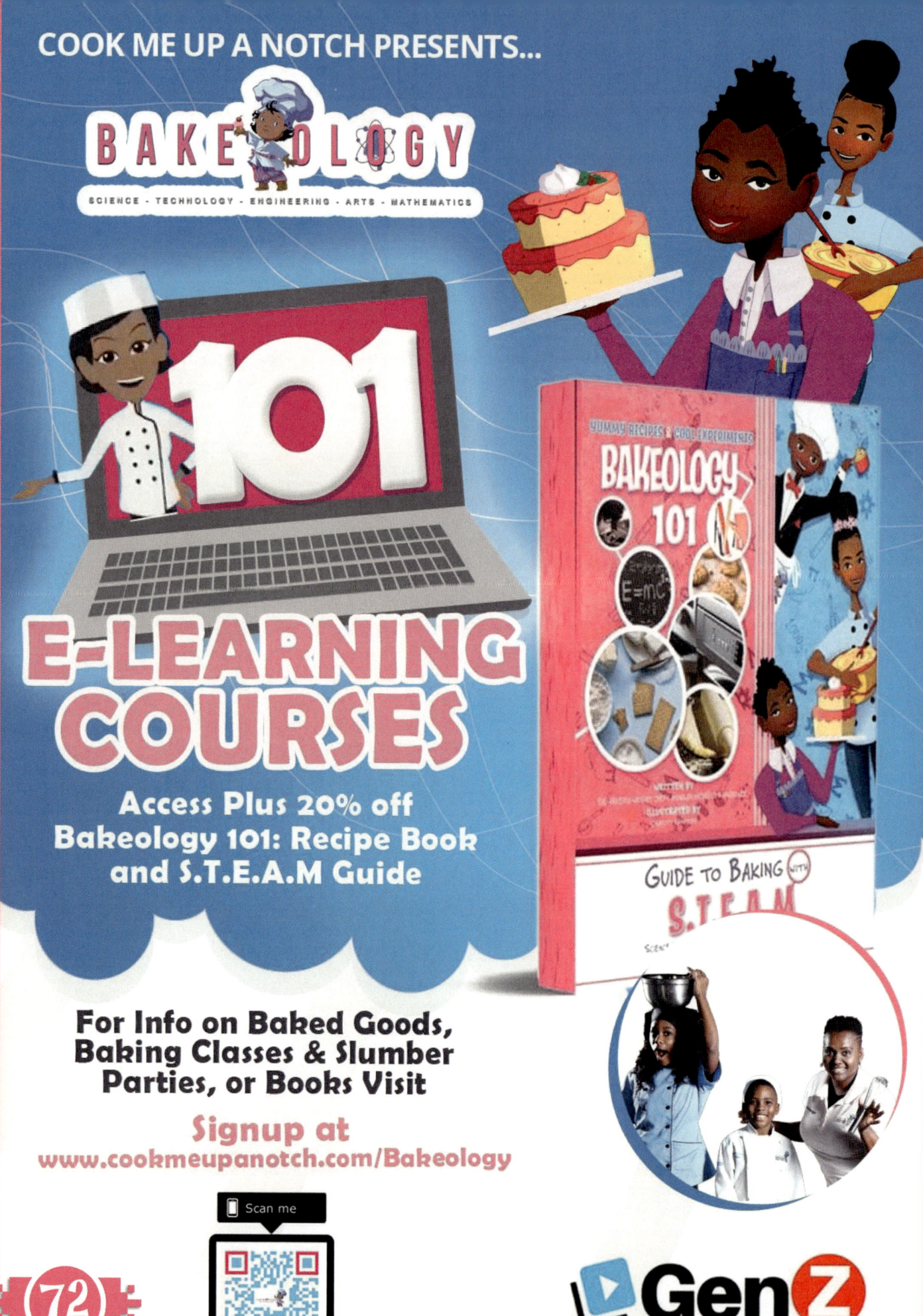

COOK ME UP A NOTCH PRESENTS...

BAKEOLOGY
SCIENCE · TECHNOLOGY · ENGINEERING · ARTS · MATHEMATICS

101 E-LEARNING COURSES

Access Plus 20% off Bakeology 101: Recipe Book and S.T.E.A.M Guide

For Info on Baked Goods, Baking Classes & Slumber Parties, or Books Visit

Signup at
www.cookmeupanotch.com/Bakeology

Scan me

72

GenZ
SOCIAL SUMMIT
A ConnectHER Media Event

Made in the USA
Columbia, SC
16 July 2019